Illustrated by George Fryer, courtesy of
Bernard Thornton Artists, London, England.

Peter Haddock Ltd., Bridlington, England.
© Peter Haddock Ltd.
Printed in Italy.

The Valiant Little Tailor

Illustrated by George Fryer

Courtesy of Bernard Thornton Artists, London, England.

SEVEN ∗ AT
ONE ∗ BLOW

One summer's morning a Tailor was sitting by his window, sewing away with all his might when down the street came a peasant woman crying, "Good preserves for sale!" This sounded good to the Tailor and he called to the woman. He looked over her jars and jampots and finally made his choice.

The woman weighed out a half-pound for him, took her money and went on her way. Taking some bread, he cut a slice and spread the jam upon it. "This will taste good," said he, "but before I sup I will finish sewing this waistcoat."

So he laid the bread down near him and
continued sewing. Meanwhile the smell of the
jam rose to the ceiling where there were many
flies and enticed them down. Soon a swarm of
them had settled on the jam. The little man flew
into a rage on seeing these unbidden guests.
Snatching up a piece of cloth, he brought it

down upon them unmercifully. When he raised it, no less than seven lay dead before him. "What a brave fellow," he said to himself. "The whole world shall hear of this." In haste he stitched a wide belt and put on it in large letters — SEVEN AT ONE BLOW. Then he bound the belt around his body and prepared to travel forth into the world.

From the cupboard he took a piece of cheese.
Outside the door he saw a bird entangled in a
bush, so he pocketed that too. Then he set off.
At the top of a high hill he found a Giant sitting
beside some rocks. "Good-day, friend," said the
little Tailor boldly. "I am on my way to see the
wide world. Would you care to join me?"

"You miserable fellow, you vagabond," said the Giant contemptuously. "That may be," answered the Tailor, "but here, you may read what sort of man I am." So saying he showed his belt with SEVEN AT ONE BLOW on it. The Giant read these words and felt a little respect for him.

But, to test the Tailor's strength, he picked up a stone and squeezed it until a few drops of water fell from it.

"Do that, if you can!" said the Giant.

The Tailor dived into his pocket, took out the cheese and squeezed it until the whey ran out. The Giant could not believe his eyes. Picking up another stone, he threw it so high that it could scarcely by seen. "Well done," said the Tailor, "but your stone must fall – and mine will not." Taking the bird from his pocket, he threw it in the air and it flew away.

"You throw well," agreed the Giant, "but can you help me carry yonder tree?" "Of course," replied the Tailor. "You take the trunk and I will carry the boughs – which are heavier." The Giant picked up the trunk, but the Tailor, knowing the Giant

could not turn to see, jumped up into the branches. When the Giant became tired and called a halt, the Tailor hopped to the ground. "You are too strong for me," gasped the Giant, when he saw the Tailor still fresh and vigorous. "Perhaps we had best go our separate ways."

The Tailor walked until he became tired and then lay down and went to sleep. When he awoke a messenger from the King — and many other people — were standing looking at the words on his belt. "Ah," they said. "He must be a great warrior and hero."

So the Tailor was taken with much
ceremony to the King who was
pleased to find such a useful man.
"In the forest," said the King, "there
live two evil Giants. If you overcome
both I will give you half my kingdom
and my daughter in marriage."

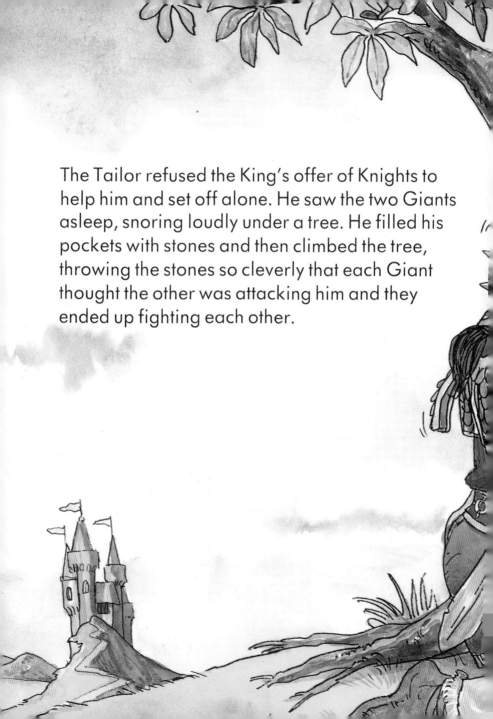

The Tailor refused the King's offer of Knights to help him and set off alone. He saw the two Giants asleep, snoring loudly under a tree. He filled his pockets with stones and then climbed the tree, throwing the stones so cleverly that each Giant thought the other was attacking him and they ended up fighting each other.

The Tailor rode back to the King to claim his reward of half the kingdom and the hand of the Princess in marriage, but the King had regretted his promise and had found another task for him. "You must capture a Unicorn from the deepest woods." Again the Tailor set out on his own. All he had with him were a rope and an axe to catch the animal.

He had only searched for a short time when the Unicorn came rushing at him. He stepped behind a tree and the horn of the Unicorn became wedged in the trunk of the tree. He used the rope to bind the Unicorn and then cut off its horn with the axe. Then he took it in triumph to the King to claim his reward.

The wedding was celebrated with much splendour and the Tailor became a Prince. But one night the Princess heard her husband talking in his sleep, saying, "Boy, stitch up these trousers, or I will lay the yardstick about your ears!" and told her father she had discovered her husband was only a Tailor.

The King said to her, "Leave the door open
tonight and, when he is fast asleep, my servants
will bind him and take him away."
However, the Tailor was warned of the plan.
That night when the Princess thought her husband
was asleep she opened the door and crept
quietly back to her bed.

But the Tailor was only pretending and said loudly, "Boy, come here and stitch these trousers or I will beat you. Seven have I killed with one blow, two Giants have I overcome and a Unicorn have I captured. How then should I be afraid of those who stand outside my bedroom door?"

At this the men fled in terror and never again did any man oppose the Valiant Little Tailor.

Thus the little Tailor became King and ruled wisely and well for many years.